WRITTEN BY
MICHAEL DAHL

Sports
Illustrated
KIDS

ILLUSTRATED BY
UDAYANA LUGO

GOODNIGHT
BASKETBALL

Snow tumbles down
from a silver-grey sky.

Cars honk their horns.
Trains rumble by.

The arena fills up with excitement and fans. Crowds enter the building and rush to the stands!

The music blares and spotlights gleam.
Look there! Our champions, our
starters, our team!

The teams circle up.
At the whistle, they jump!

The tip off is ours!
The players are pumped!

When half-time is over
the players get serious!
That ball really zooms!
It's fast and it's furious!

More passes and dribbles –
three-pointers galore!
Both teams are so good
that they even the score.

The crowd goes wild!
The game has been won!

In the arena behind us,
they turn off the lights.

Now it's time to go home
and say our goodnights.

Goodnight
basketball,

goodnight
court. . . .

Goodnight to the teams of my favourite sport!

Goodnight to the hoops
and benches and stands!

Goodnight to the mascots! Goodnight to the fans!

Goodnight,
new friends.
"See you next time,"
they say.

Goodnight to
the trains that
we travelled
on today.

Here's our stop.
There's my home.
What a game!
What a day!
Now it's time to put
everything away.

Goodnight,
favourite jersey.
Goodnight,
favourite shoes.

Goodnight to all players, win or lose. . . .

Goodnight, superstars,
shining so bright.
Now it's time to turn off the light.

Goodnight, basketball. . . .
Goodnight.

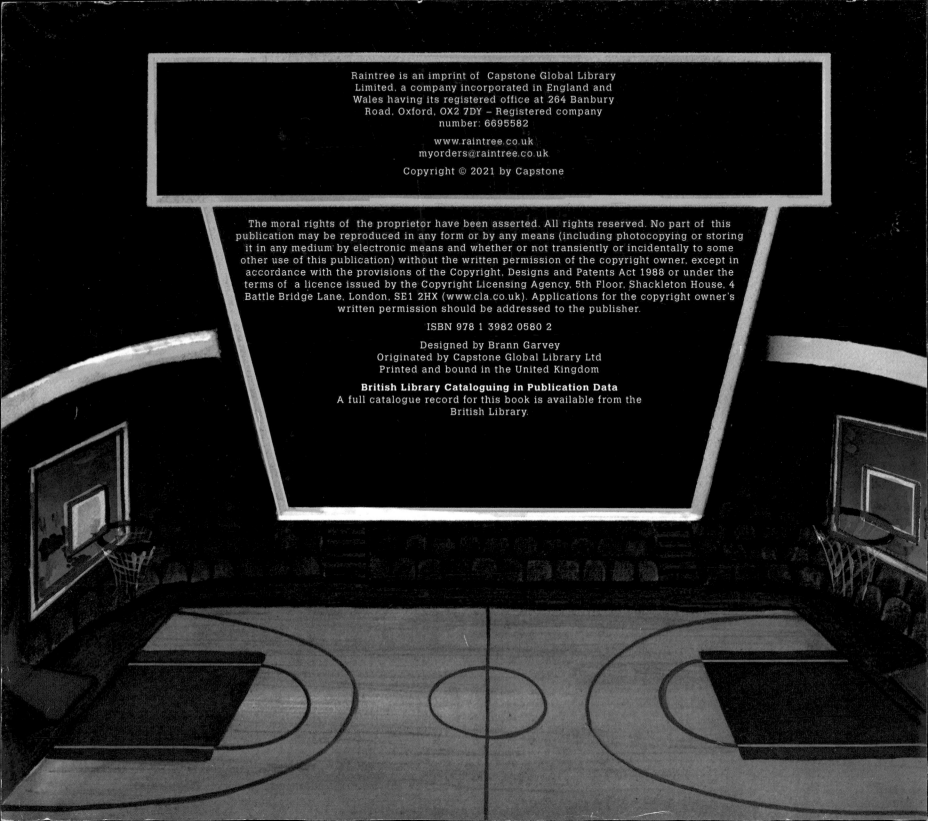

Raintree is an imprint of Capstone Global Library
Limited, a company incorporated in England and
Wales having its registered office at 264 Banbury
Road, Oxford, OX2 7DY – Registered company
number: 6695582

www.raintree.co.uk
myorders@raintree.co.uk

ISBN 978 1 3982 0580 2

Designed by Brann Garvey
Originated by Capstone Global Library Ltd
Printed and bound in the United Kingdom

British Library Cataloguing in Publication Data
A full catalogue record for this book is available from the
British Library.